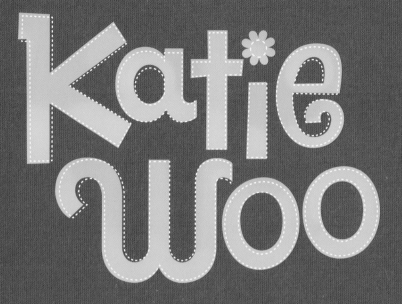

Katie's Spooky Sleepover

by Fran Manushkin

illustrated by Tammie Lyon

PICTURE WINDOW BOOKS
a capstone imprint

Katie Woo is published by Picture Window Books,
A Capstone Imprint
1710 Roe Crest Drive
North Mankato, Minnesota 56003
www.mycapstone.com

Text © 2017 Fran Manushkin
Illustrations © 2017 Picture Window Books

Library of Congress Cataloging-in-Publication Data
Names: Manushkin, Fran, author. | Lyon, Tammie, illustrator. |
    Manushkin, Fran. Katie Woo.
Title: Katie's spooky sleepover / by Fran Manushkin ; [illustrator,
    Tammie Lyon].
Description: North Mankato, Minnesota : Picture Window Books, an
    imprint of Capstone Press, [2017] | Series: Katie Woo | Summary:
    Katie's friends have come for a sleepover, and telling a scary story
    seems like a good idea—until she has a dream about a monster under
    her bed, and she wakes up to find her lucky kimono missing.
Identifiers: LCCN 2016017940| ISBN 9781479596409 (library binding) |
    ISBN 9781479596423 (pbk.) | ISBN 9781479596447 (ebook pdf)
Subjects: LCSH: Woo, Katie (Fictitious character)—Juvenile fiction. |
    Chinese Americans—Juvenile fiction. | Kimonos—Juvenile fiction. |
    Sleepovers—Juvenile fiction. | Storytelling—Juvenile fiction. |
    Friendship—Juvenile fiction. | CYAC: Chinese Americans—Fiction. |
    Kimonos—Fiction. | Sleepovers—Fiction. | Storytelling—Fiction. |
    Friendship—Fiction.
Classification: LCC PZ7.M3195 Kcu 2017 | DDC 813.54 [E]—dc23
LC record available at https://lccn.loc.gov/2016017940

Graphic Designer: Heidi Thompson
Photo Credits:
Greg Holch, pg. 26
Tammie Lyon, pg. 26
Vector images, Shutterstock ©

Printed in the United States of America in North Mankato, Minnesota.
009665F16

Table of Contents

Chapter 1
Sleepover Fun

Katie was having a

sleepover.

Mattie and JoJo came

with their pj's and their

favorite dolls.

Janie, a new friend, said,

"This is my first sleepover."

"Sleepovers are fun!" said

Katie. "You'll see."

"First we eat," said Katie.

"Pizza is the best!" said Mattie.

"No!" yelled JoJo.

"Cupcakes are!"

"Now let's play dress-up and make fancy hats," said Katie.

"Yay, pom-poms!" said Mattie.

"Fuzzy feathers!" yelled JoJo.

"Shiny sparkles!" said Janie.

"Look at my fancy kimono," said Katie. "My dad got it in Japan. He says it's lucky."

Everyone wanted to try it on.

Then they put on their

pj's and arranged their

sleeping bags in a circle.

"We all have flowers,"

said Janie. "Katie's room

looks like a garden."

Chapter 2

Things Get Spooky

Soon it was getting dark.

"How about a ghost story?"

said Mattie. "I love them."

"Great!" said Katie. She

turned off the lights.

Mattie held a flashlight
under her chin.

"Yikes!" yelled Janie. "Your
face looks spooky!"

"My story is spooky too,"
said Mattie.

Mattie began. "Once upon a time, there was a monster. It had a big bony finger, and it went around the world poking people."

JoJo snuck up and poked

Janie.

"Help!" she yelled. "It's

the monster!"

"It's me!" JoJo laughed.

"Now I'm worried," said Janie. "Maybe there are monsters here."

"No way!" insisted Katie. "There are no monsters in my house!"

But that night, Katie

had a spooky dream. She

dreamed that a monster was

under her bed!

Chapter 3
Where's Katie's Kimono?

Katie woke up early, still thinking about her spooky dream.

"I'll put on my lucky kimono," she decided. "That will help me feel better."

But her kimono was gone!

"Oh, no!" said Katie.

"Maybe there is a monster

under my bed. And he took

my kimono."

Janie was still asleep, but
Mattie and JoJo were awake.
Katie told them about the
monster.

"We have to look under
your bed," said Mattie.

Mattie and Katie and JoJo

were scared. But they held hands

and looked under the bed.

"Yikes!" yelled Mattie.

"Something poked me."

"It's the monster!" yelled
Katie and JoJo.

"Surprise!" yelled Janie.
"It's me."

"That was funny," said
Katie. "And you have my
kimono!"

"I was scared," explained
Janie, "and I didn't have
my teddy bear. So I put
on your lucky kimono. It
really helped."

"I'm glad," Katie said.

Then the girls got another
surprise.

"Guess what's for
breakfast?" said Katie's mom.
"Ghost pancakes."

"Wow!" joked JoJo. "More
spooks!"

Janie said, "This is the best sleepover!"

"For sure!" agreed Mattie and JoJo.

"Now," said Katie, "let's make the last ghost disappear."

And they shared the last pancake.

About the Author

Fran Manushkin is the author of many popular picture books, including *Happy in Our Skin*; *Baby, Come Out!*; *Latkes and Applesauce: A Hanukkah Story*; *The Tushy Book*; *The Belly Book*; and *Big Girl Panties*. There is a real Katie Woo — she's Fran's great-niece — but she never gets in half the trouble of the Katie Woo in the books. Fran writes on her beloved Mac computer in New York City, without the help of her two naughty cats, Chaim and Goldy.

About the Illustrator

Tammie Lyon began her love for drawing at a young age while sitting at the kitchen table with her dad. She continued her love of art and eventually attended the Columbus College of Art and Design, where she earned a bachelor's degree in fine art. After a brief career as a professional ballet dancer, she decided to devote herself full time to illustration. Today she lives with her husband, Lee, in Cincinnati, Ohio. Her dogs, Gus and Dudley, keep her company as she works in her studio.

Glossary

arrange (uh-RAYNJ)—to place in an order

disappear (diss-uh-GREE)—to go out of sight or go missing

fancy (FAN-see)—not plain

favorite (FAY-vuh-rit)—the person or thing you like best

garden (GAR-duhn)—a place where flowers, vegetables, and shrubs are grown

kimono (kuh-MOH-nuh)—a long, loose robe with wide sleeves and a sash, worn in Japan

shiny (SHY-nee)—very smooth and bright

Discussion Questions

1. What activities did the girls do at Katie's sleepover? What kinds of things would you do at a sleepover?

2. It was Janie's first sleepover. How do you think she felt? How did you feel at your first sleepover?

3. Katie, Mattie, and JoJo looked under Katie's bed to see if a monster was there. What would you see if you looked under your bed?

Writing Prompts

1. Mattie told a scary story about a monster who went around the world poking people. Write your own scary story.

2. Katie has a lucky kimono her dad got her in Japan. Draw a picture of something you have that's lucky.

3. Make a list of the food that the girls ate at the sleepover. Then make a list of three of your favorite foods.

Katie Woo's Super Stylish Contest Winners

Katie's kimono in this book was designed by a Katie Woo reader as part of a nationwide contest! This winning entry stood out for its creativity.

Kate Lin, grade 2, South Grove Elementary School
Syosset, New York

Cooking with Katie Woo!

You can make your own ghost pancakes for a super spooky breakfast! Just make sure to ask a grown-up for help.

Ghost Pancakes

What you need:

- your favorite pancake mix

- a few chocolate chips or blueberries

- syrup

Other things you need:

- large mixing bowl

- whisk

- large nonstick skillet

- spatula

What you do:

1. In the large mixing bowl, use the whisk to mix your pancake batter according to the instructions on the box.

2. Heat a large nonstick skillet over medium-high heat.

3. Spread the pancake batter onto your skillet in ghostly shapes.

4. Place two chocolate chips or blueberries on the pancake for eyes and one for a mouth.

5. Cook until it's bubbly on top. Then flip with the spatula and cook the other side.

6. Top with syrup, and enjoy!

THE FUN DOESN'T STOP HERE!

Discover more at www.capstonekids.com

- ♥ Videos & Contests
- ❁ Games & Puzzles
- ♥ Friends & Favorites
- ❁ Authors & Illustrators

Find cool websites and more books like this one at www.facthound.com. Just type in the Book ID: **9781479596409** and you're ready to go!

12/16